I waited in the silence of the ocean's depths. I waited for the wind and the
storm, I waited for the delicate foam that would carry me straight to you, the wave
that would set me down on your hot sand.
I waited . . .

I wanted to meet you—to be a boomerang, take the time to get to know your fingers,
to travel a little from you to you. A boomerang? Why not?
We found each other.
And I saw the Milky Way. To go up there, what a magnificent
adventure! Like you, I have so many things to discover.

STAR FISH, I DREAMT I WAS A STAR IN THE SKY.

Leave!
How could I leave?
I left.
I didn't want to cause you pain.
Your tears are salty but the sky is blue, I want to soar in it. The night is
dark, I will brighten it. Don't forget to look at me.

Good-bye.

I will dive back into my ocean, bathe in its silence.
I will no longer hear the cormorants, the seagulls, nor the boats' sirens
or the lap of the waves . . .
You are gone, you grew up . . .
I will think about your smile for a long time.
I have come home. I am a star.

—Hubert Michel
    (Translated by Emily van Beek)

Antonin Louchard

Little Star

Hyperion Books for Children
New York

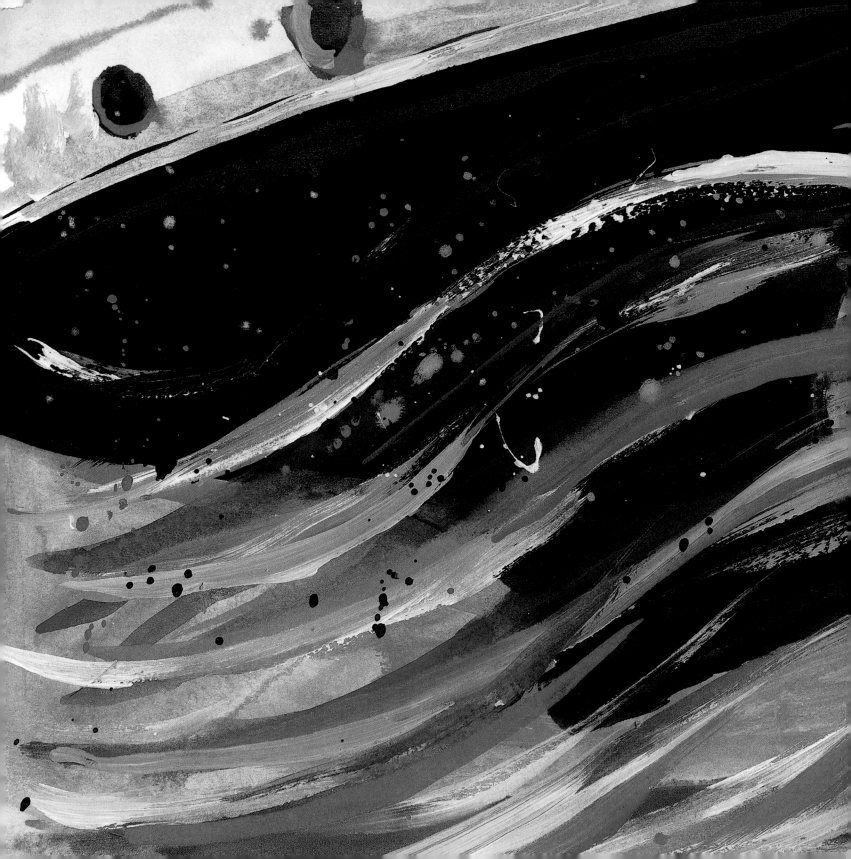

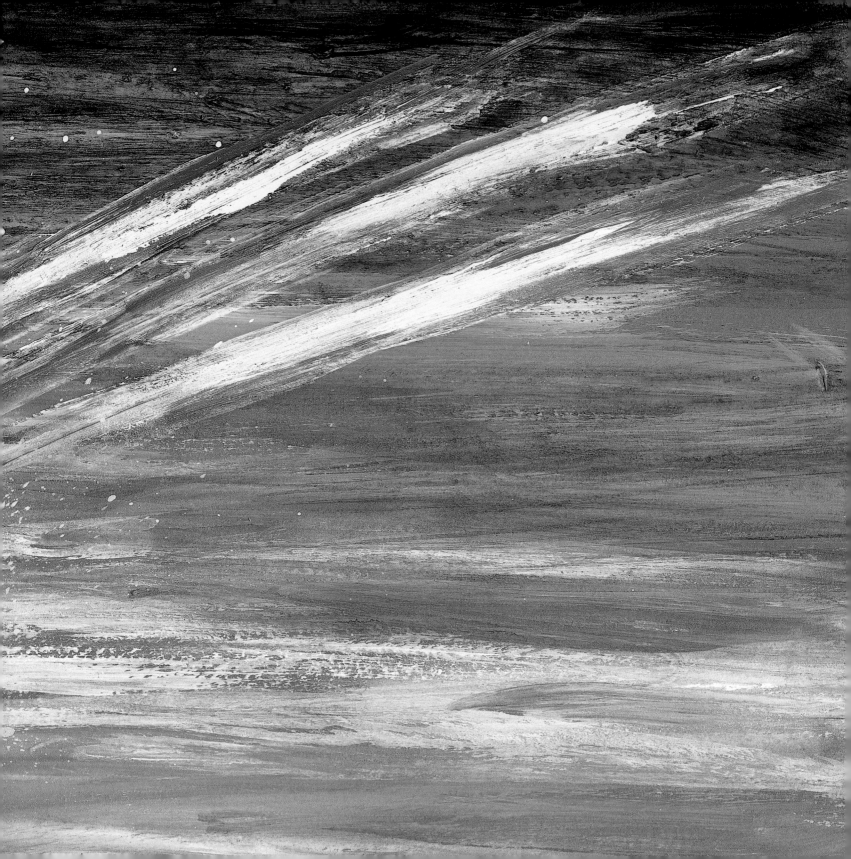

For Carla

First published by Gallimard Jeunesse / Giboulées
First U.S. Edition, 2003
1 3 5 7 9 10 8 6 4 2

Printed in Singapore

Library of Congress Cataloging-in-Publication Data on file.
ISBN 0-7868-1939-1

Visit www.hyperionchildrensbooks.com